THE NIGHT BEFORE CHRISTMAS

BY CLEMENT ♠ C. ♠ MOORE L.L.D.
ILLUSTRATED by RICHARD JESSE WATSON

HarperCollins Publishers

'Twas the night before Christmas,

when all through the house

not a creature was stirring,

not even a mouse.

The stockings were hung

by the chimney with care,

in hopes that St. Nicholas

soon would be there.

The children were nestled

all snug in their beds,

while visions of sugarplums

danced in their heads.

And Ma in her kerchief

and I in my cap

had just settled our brains

for a long winter's nap

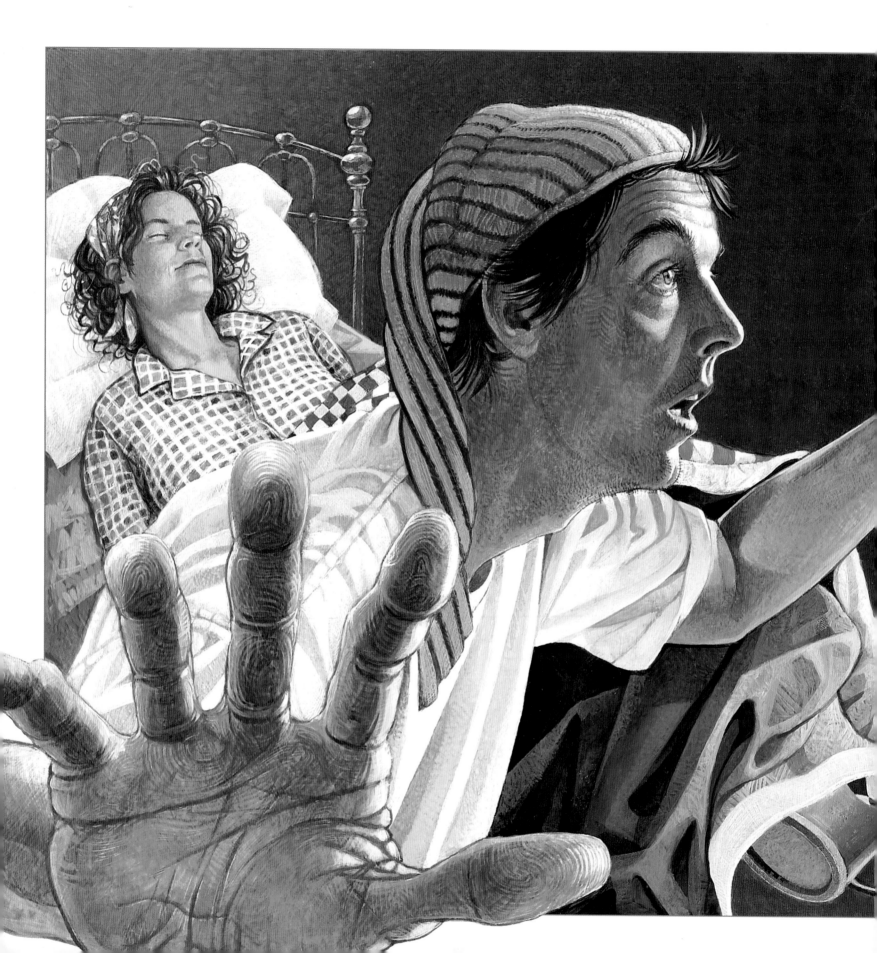

When out on the lawn
there arose such a clatter,
I sprang from the bed
to see what was the matter.
Away to the window
I flew like a flash,
tore open the shutters,
and threw up the sash.

The moon on the breast

of the new-fallen snow

gave the lustre of midday

to objects below,

when what to my wondering

eyes should appear

but a miniature sleigh

and eight tiny reindeer,

With a little old driver

so lively and quick,

I knew in a moment

it must be St. Nick.

More rapid than eagles

his coursers they came,

and he whistled and shouted

and called them by name:

"Now, Dasher! now, Dancer! now, Prancer and Vixen!
On, Comet! on, Cupid! on, Donder and Blitzen!

To the top of the porch! to the top of the wall!

Now, dash away! Dash away! Dash away all!"

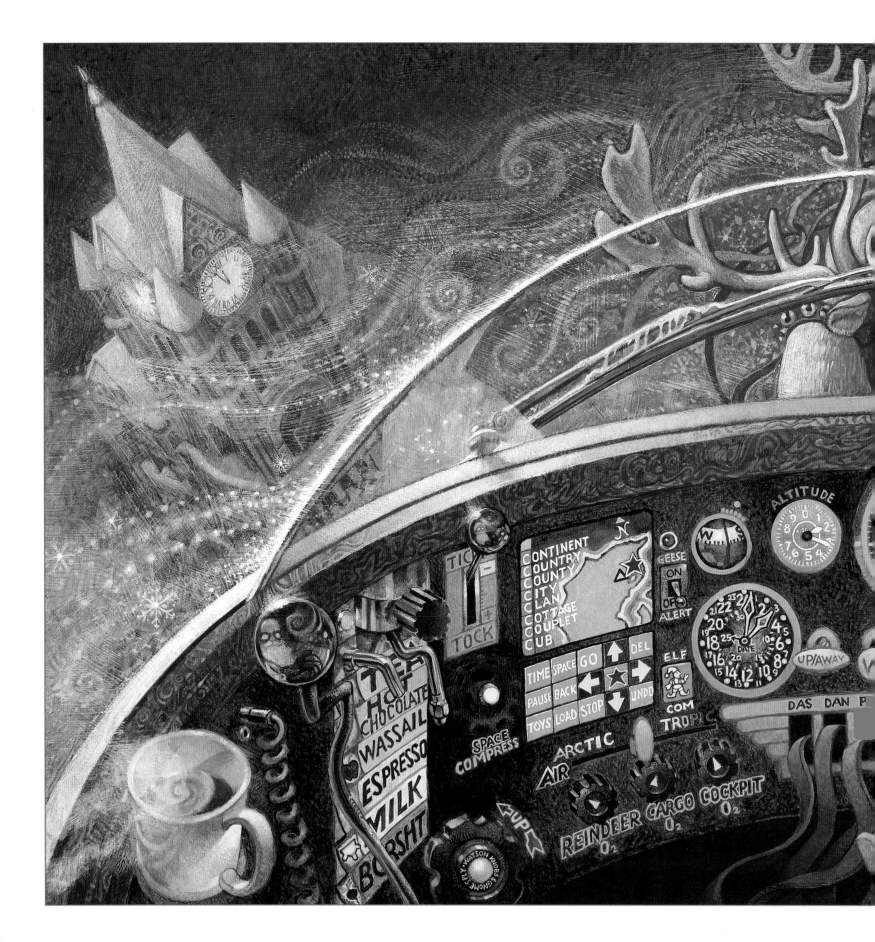

As dry leaves that before

the wild hurricane fly,

when they meet with an obstacle,

mount to the sky,

so up to the housetop

the coursers they flew,

with the sleigh full of toys,

and St. Nicholas too.

And then, in a twinkling,

I heard on the roof

the prancing and pawing

of each little hoof.

As I drew in my head

and was turning around,

down the chimney St. Nicholas

came with a bound.

He was dressed all in fur,
from his head to his foot,
and his clothes were all tarnished
with ashes and soot.
A bundle of toys
he had flung on his back,
and he looked like a peddler
just opening his pack.

His eyes, how they twinkled!

His dimples, how merry!

His cheeks were like roses,

his nose like a cherry!

His droll little mouth

was drawn up like a bow,

and the beard of his chin

was as white as the snow.

The stump of a pipe
he held tight in his teeth,
and the smoke, it encircled
his head like a wreath.
He had a broad face
and a little round belly
that shook, when he laughed,
like a bowlful of jelly.

He was chubby and plump,

a right jolly old elf,

and I laughed when I saw him,

in spite of myself.

A wink of his eye

and a twist of his head

soon gave me to know

I had nothing to dread.

He spoke not a word,
but went straight to his work
and filled all the stockings,
then turned with a jerk,
and laying his finger
aside of his nose,
and giving a nod,
up the chimney he rose.

He sprang to his sleigh,

to his team gave a whistle,

and away they all flew

like the down of a thistle.

But I heard him exclaim,

ere he drove out of sight,

"Merry Christmas
to all,
and to all
a Good Night!"

Q & A WITH ST. NICK

The following interview between St. Nick and Richard Jesse Watson took place
at the Port Townsend Tyler Street Coffee House shortly after Christmas.

WATSON: Let me say, first of all, what an honor it is to finally meet you.

ST. NICK: Oh! Ho! Ho! Ho! You know, Richard, I have seen you on
many occasions, but you were always asleep. Except that one time—

WATSON: Oh, my gosh! You have got a good memory. Heh, heh.
Well . . . so what do you like to be called?

ST. NICK: Slim.

WATSON: I beg your pardon?

ST. NICK: Ha! Ha! Ho! Ho! Just kidding. No, that really depends on where
I am on the Big Blue Marble. Some call me St. Nicholas, Father
Christmas, Santa Claus, Kris Kringle, or Kris. Up North, I'm called The
Wandering One, Pihoqahiaq, an Inuit name for polar bear. The missus
calls me Punkins. Take your pick.

WATSON: Okaay. . . . Ah, Nicholas, everyone's big question: How do
you deliver so much to so many all in one night?

ST. NICK: So you want to know the secret to the Big Milk and
Cookie Run? It's simple: eight svelte reindeer and a special
customized sleigh.

WATSON: Tell me about your reindeer.

ST. NICK: Oh, they're the best. Each one has so much heart. They were a gift, you know, from the king and queen of Lapland one year while I was visiting during Candlemas. Lovely couple, excellent dancers.

WATSON: You are, of course, a Master Toymaker, but it's rumored that you are also a legendary reindeer whisperer.

ST. NICK: That's true. I do love animals. I developed a special reindeer feed made from Austrian edelweiss, Canadian lichen, Norwegian oats, Finnish glacial milk, Russian bee pollen, Swedish cloudberries, and solar flare. A concoction such as this stimulates their ability to move fast. Very fast.

WATSON: Absolutely incredible! So then, your sleigh—

ST. NICK: Ah, yes. The Polaris is composed of high- and low-tech materials, such as foam titanium and comet dust. This baby is tricked out with electron injection and a little old gamma ray booster I picked up at JPL Surplus in Pasadena. By tucking in the wishes and hopes of children everywhere, the sleigh is able to expand the moment between "tick" and "tock" on Christmas Eve. Oh, it's also equipped with pontoons in case of water landing.

WATSON: Wow.

ST. NICK: Ho! Ho! Ho! Well, it's really modern science and ancient art stretched and pulled together like Christmas taffy.

WATSON: Any other thoughts?

ST. NICK: MERRY CHRISTMAS TO ALL, AND TO ALL A GOOD NIGHT!

For Betty Bea

Special thanks to Santa's helpers:

Excellent elf editor, Maria Modugno; loving elf wife, Susi; my elf children, Jesse, Mariah, Faith, John, Ben; grandelves, Clay, Jackson, Taj, Kerith, Kaylen; the real St. Nick; Maitland Hardyman & Alfred; artist elves and friends Max Grover, Frank Samuelson, Gary Peterson, Gordon C. Redmond, Jennifer Jane Yawman, Mark Chidester, Kathie Meyer & Larry the cat; Michael, Lisa, Emily, Avery & Eli Biskup; Carole Yates, Rick Halverson, Camilla Carraher, Frendl, Amy Irene Clark, Richard & Susan Thomas, Frank Ross Photographic, Port Townsend Aero Museum, Olympic Game Farm.

The Night Before Christmas

Illustrations and interview copyright © 2006 by Richard Jesse Watson • Manufactured in China. All rights reserved. No part of this book may be used or reproduced in any manner whatsoever without written permission except in the case of brief quotations embodied in critical articles and reviews. For information address HarperCollins Children's Books, a division of HarperCollins Publishers, 10 East 53rd Street, New York, NY 10022 • www.harpercollinschildrens.com

Library of Congress Cataloging-in-Publication Data

Moore, Clement Clarke, 1779-1863. The night before Christmas / by Clement C. Moore ; illustrated by Richard Jesse Watson.— 1st ed.   p.   cm. ISBN 978-0-06-075741-0 (trade bdg.) — ISBN 978-0-06-075742-7 (lib. bdg.) — ISBN 978-0-06-075744-1 (pbk.)

1. Santa Claus—Juvenile poetry. 2. Christmas—Juvenile poetry. 3. Children's poetry, American. I. Watson, Richard Jesse, ill. II. Title. PS2429.M5N5 2006b 2005028663 811'.2—dc22 CIP AC

Design by Stephanie Bart-Horvath • Hand lettering by David Coulson

❖ First Edition

09 10 11 12 13 SCP 10 9 8 7 6 5